W9-CPD-185

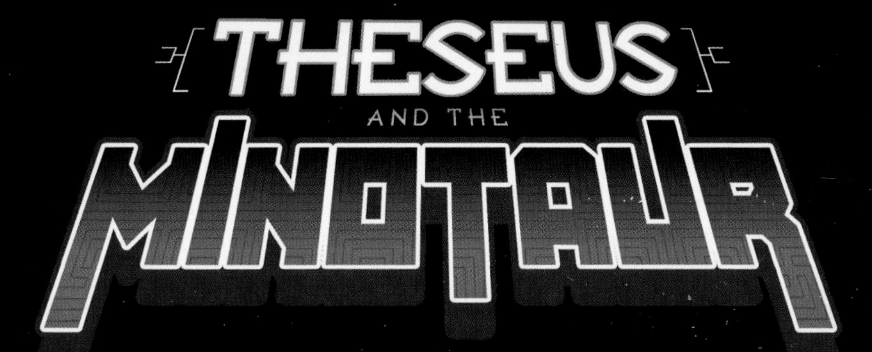

retold by Nel Yomtov
illustrated by Tod Smith
color by Dave Gutierrez

STONE ARCH BOOKS
MINNEAPOLIS SAN DIEGO

Graphic Revolve is published by Stone Arch Books
151 Good Counsel Drive, P.O. Box 669
Mankato, Minnesota 56002
www.stonearchbooks.com

Library of Congress Cataloging-in-Publication Data
Yomtov, Nel.
Theseus and the Minotaur / by Nel Yomtov; illustrated by Tod Smith.
p. cm. — (Graphic Revolve)
ISBN 978-1-4342-1171-2 (library binding)
ISBN 978-1-4342-1387-7 (pbk.)
1. Theseus (Greek mythology)—Juvenile literature. 2. Theseus (Greek mythology)—Comic books, strips, etc. 3. Minotaur (Greek mythology)—Juvenile literature. 4. Minotaur (Greek mythology)—Comic books, strips, etc. 5. Graphic novels I. Smith, Tod. II. Title.
BL820.T5Y66 2009
741.5'973—dc22 2008032066

Summary: The evil king of Crete demands that fourteen young Athenians be fed to the Minotaur, a half-man, half-bull. Only Prince Theseus can save them from the fearsome monster that lives deep in the maze-like Labyrinth.

Creative Director: Heather Kindseth
Designer: Bob Lentz

1 2 3 4 5 6 14 13 12 11 10 09

Printed in the United States of America

TABLE OF CONTENTS

INTRODUCING...

THE MINOTAUR
MEDEA

CHAPTER 1: AN HEIR TO THE THRONE
Thousands of years ago, in the town of Delphi, Greece . . .
But I must know. Will I ever —
Have a son? What good will this knowledge do you?
I must know if I will have an heir to my throne in Athens.

Go to Medea the Sorceress.
Her magic will bring you a son.
Thank you, Oracle.
But beware, foolish king. This son born of sorcery will bring you great unhappiness!

To the sorceress Medea in Corinth!
Faster, faster!
Hours later . . .
Medea's castle!
How can I help you, my lord?
I can offer you great riches, Medea, if only –

I know that you want a son, Aegeus. And a son you shall have.
But promise that you will keep me safe in Athens if I ever need your help.
Of course, Medea. I will protect you.
Then listen. The next woman you hold in your arms will bear you a son.

May the gods shine on you, Medea.
Have a safe journey, Aegeus.

On his way back to Athens, Aegeus visited a friend in the city of Troezen . . .
I am filled with happiness to see you again, Pittheus.
Your daughter, Aethra, is as beautiful as a goddess.
Time for us to find her a good husband!
Don't be foolish, Father.
May I refill your cup, my lord?
Oh! I'm sorry!
Let me clean this up.

Ooh!
I've got you! No harm done, child!
The next morning . . .
I've left a gift for you under the boulder in your garden.
It is for the son I hope you will one day have.
Please let this be our secret.
A son? What could he mean?

Many years passed, but King Aegeus finally had a son . . .
You are a lively one, boy!

. . . but not the son that the oracle had promised.
Medea, my queen. Our son grows stronger every day.
And handsome, like his father, husband.

"You kept your word, Aegeus. You protected me and gave me shelter when my enemies came for me."
"We became man and wife. And our son, Medus, is heir to the throne."
You've made me the happiest man in the city, Medea.
And I am the happiest woman . . .
. . . because one day my son will be king of Athens.

CHAPTER 2: THESEUS THE BOLD
In nearby Troezen . . .
What manner of household is this . . .
. . . when a guest arrives and he is not properly greeted?!
Come here, Theseus!
Hercules! I've been waiting for you!

How are you, Aunt Aethra?
Fine, my nephew.
But my Theseus thinks only about fighting and having big muscles like you.
Have you told the boy who his father is?
He has the right to know.
I will tell him — at the right time.
What does he mean mother?
Tell me!
See what you've started, Hercules.
Away with you, now!
You are right, Hercules. But when will the right time come to tell Theseus?

Ten years passed . . .
Go, Theseus! You've got 'em!
You're the best, Theseus!
And the most handsome, isn't he, Aethra?
Run away! He's back!!
Periphetes is coming! Everyone run!
Again?!
No! Today we stop running from him!

You'd better start running, little man.
I'm done running!
And you're not welcome here!
Ooompph!!
SMASH!!

Unnhh.
Got it!
SLAMMM!!

Your clubbing days are over, Periphetes!
Theseus, hero of Troezen!
Only you could have stopped him!
Nice going, Theseus!
The time has come for him to know the truth about his father.

Let's go home. I want you to do something.
Lift it, Theseus! Try harder!
Underneath you'll find the gifts that your father left for you.

Your father is Aegeus, King of Athens.
What?

And the time has come for you to go to him.

He will be happy to see you, but he doesn't even know you're alive.
My father's a king!
Go to Athens by boat. It is safer. The road is filled with many dangers.
No, Mother.
I'll go by road, and make the gods take notice of my brave deeds.

CHAPTER 3: THE DANGEROUS ROAD

Having done another brave deed, Theseus set off again toward Athens.

Days later, Theseus entered a strange village with houses built on poles . . .
You there! Why are you running?
Look out behind you!
The boar is coming!
What?!
SNORT!

Theseus did not hesitate . . .
SMACK!
CRACKK!!
That was easy enough.
I wonder what other dangers lie ahead . . .

Later, while walking along the cliffs of Megara . . .
Ah! Another victim — I mean, traveler!
Tie my sandals, and I will let you pass.
Are you finished yet, boy?
Y-yes, Sciron.
TAP! TAP! TAP!
Then let me help you on your way!
Noooooo!

SPLASH!!
Help me, Sciron! Please!
SNAP!!

By the gods!
Hey, you!
If you want to use my road, you must pay the toll.
Come and tie my sandals.
Stand aside, old man.
Do you want to join the one below, youngster?!
Aha!
WHOOSH!
And again!
WHOOSH!!

Ungh!
Your time has come, Sciron . . .
. . . now you must pay the toll!
Nooo!
Another villain falls at the hands of Theseus!

CHAPTER 4: THE POISON CUP
Theseus finally reached Athens . . .
Such a grand city!
That must be Theseus!
Yes, the one who sent Sciron and the others to their deaths!
Medea was in the crowd that day . . .
My powers tell me that is Theseus, son of Aegeus!
When Aegeus learns that Theseus was born, he will make him the prince . . .

. . . and my son, Medus, will never be king of Athens.
I will not let that happen!
Back to the palace! Quickly!

Later, at King Aegeus's palace . . .
My powers tell me that the blond-haired stranger is a spy . . .
. . . sent here to kill you!
A spy?!
Yes, but I have a plan.
I will send guards to find the stranger.
They will invite him to tonight's feast.

We'll give him a room and fresh clothing.
We'll treat him royally.
Just before the feast, I will put a poison in his drink.
And then?
You will have our guests drink to his health.
When he drinks, he will die instantly . . .
. . . and that will be the end of him.

Later, at the banquet . . .
I can't wait to tell Aegeus that I am his son!
Although we've just met, I feel I've known you all your life.
Let us drink to our brave, young guest.
To your good health — what?!
M-my sword!

No! Don't drink!
Huh?!
Only one person in this world could have my sword.
Are you — ?
Yes, Father, I am your son, Theseus.
Finally you are by my side.
Forget Medea. I will deal with her later.
Come, we have much to talk about, son.

Time passed, and Prince Theseus performed many brave deeds.
But none were braver than slaying the giant white bull.
The huge creature was the son of Poseidon, the god of the sea.

The bull had terrorized all of Greece for many years.
King Ageus sent many men to slay the great beast . . . and just as many had been killed.
On the day that Theseus killed the bull . . .
There is much you need to know about the fierce bull . . .
. . . and the pain it has brought to the people of Athens.

One of the soldiers I sent to fight the bull was the son of King Minos of Crete.
Minos's son was killed by the creature.
Then, Minos's wife gave birth to a second son.
The child had the chest and arms of a man . . .
. . . but the head and legs of a bull.
It was named the Minotaur.

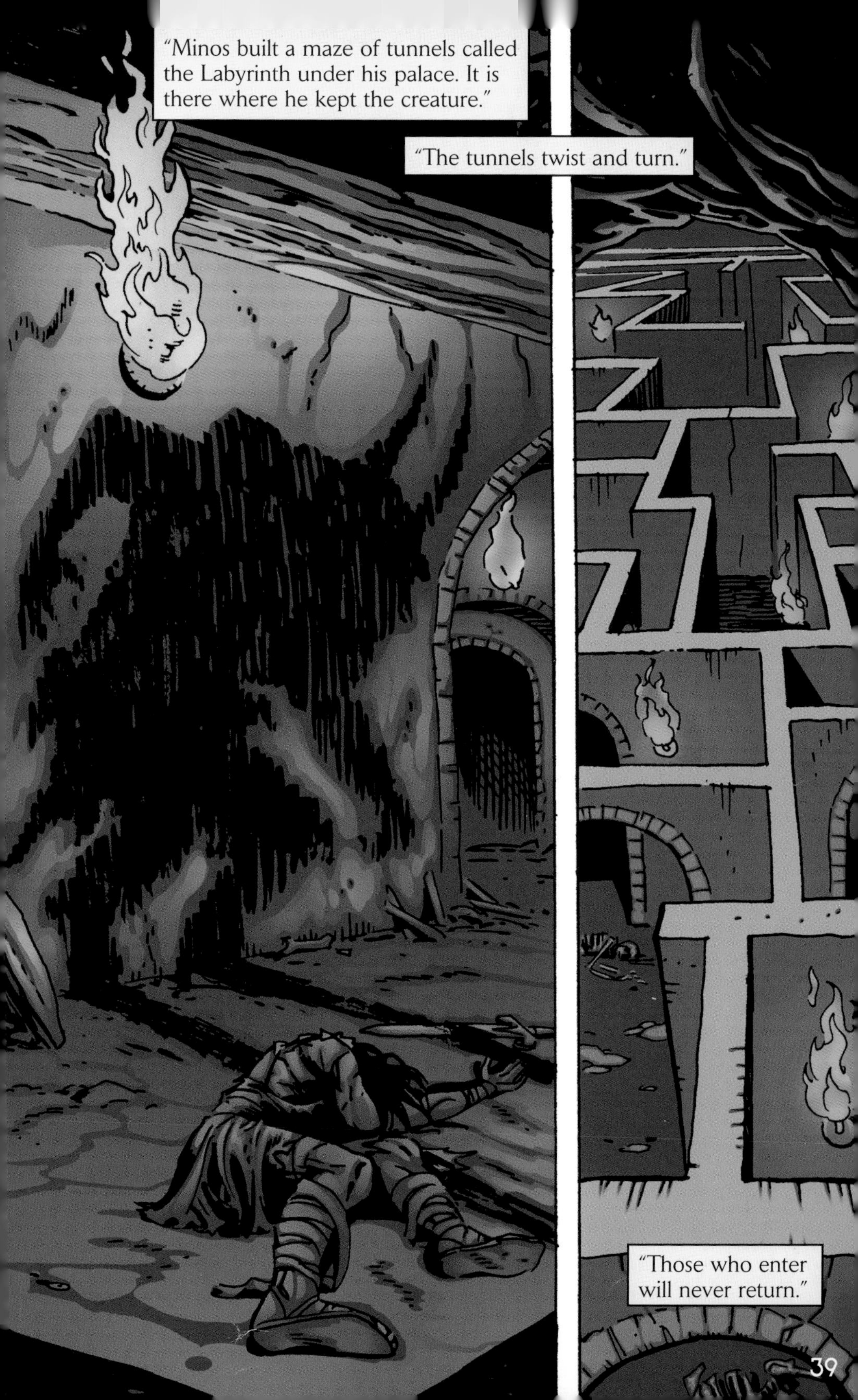
"Minos built a maze of tunnels called the Labyrinth under his palace. It is there where he kept the creature."
"The tunnels twist and turn."
"Those who enter will never return."

What does this have to do with us?
In a few days, fourteen youths from Athens will be sent to Crete . . .
. . . and fed to the Minotaur!
But why?!
Minos blames me for his son's death.
As punishment, he makes us sacrifice our children.
And if we refuse?
His army will crush Athens.
Then I will travel to Crete and destroy the Minotaur!
No! You will never return alive!
I swear I will succeed, father.

I am the prince of Athens! I must save my people.
Perhaps you are right. But one more thing . . .
The ship you will take to Crete has a black sail . . .
Take a white sail with you. Use it when you return.
When I see your white sail from the cliffs, I will know that you are alive and have succeeded.
Yes, Father. I'll go prepare for my journey right away.
May the gods forgive me if my dear son is killed.

CHAPTER 5: THE MINOTAUR!
The ship's fourteen unlucky youths sailed for Crete . . .
. . . where they were to be fed to the Minotaur.
Days later, the ship arrived in Crete. King Minos was there to meet Theseus.
You wanted to see the famous prince of Athens, Ariadne.
Is he everything you expected, daughter?

Well, father, I . . .
Get a good look at your handsome stranger now.
Tomorrow he will be the Minotaur's dinner!
Get them out of my sight, and take them to their cells!

The next night in the Labyrinth . . .
I've led these poor souls to their deaths. I have failed my father.
Psst, Theseus!

Princess!
Shhh. I've come to help you escape.
But promise me one thing . . .
. . . take me with you and make me your wife.
Of course.
Then listen carefully.

I'll tie one end here. Carry the rest with you.
The string will unwind as you go through the maze.
To get out, follow the trail of string back here.
I hear my father coming. I must go.
I'll meet you back here later. Good luck, my love.
I've decided to send you into the Labyrinth first, Theseus!
Take him away!
Good luck, Athenian! Hah hah!

Those sounds must be the Minotaur!
Good thing it's so dark here . . .
URNWHH
. . . or the guards would have seen the string.

The others will be sent in after the Minotaur's done with you!
URNHH

The beast's growls grow louder.
URNNHH
And I can smell his foul odor.
URNNHH

URNNHH
I can feel the Minotaur near me . . .
By the gods!

URNHH!!
URNHH!
URNHH

HRNNGGH!!
THWACK!!
RRRRRRRRRR

THWACK!!
BAMM!!!
Just missed me!

SLAMM!!
FWACK!!
WHAMM!!!
Can't take this beating much longer . . .
That torch gives me an idea.

GRONKK!
Made it!
WRONKK!!

Unhh!
GRONKK!
Unnh! Got to keep pulling!
WRONKK!!
Yes!!
KRACKK!!
KRASHH!!

Now to free the others.
Hmm. Those guards are in my way. . .

KRONG!!
KRONG!!
KRONG!!
Ariadne! Take their key and free my friends! Quickly!
This is the fastest way back to your ship! Hurry!

At the harbor . . .
I promised you freedom, my love, and now you must take me with you.
Y-yes, of course.
What have I done? I don't love Ariadne.
Why did I make such a foolish promise?

CHAPTER 6: THE BLACK SAIL

Prepare to sail! We're leaving immediately!
Minutes later . . .
The ship is sailing? But why?!
Theseus! Theseus!
Curse you, Theseus! I loved you more than anything!
I only wanted to clean the white sail for you, and now you've abandoned me!

Days later, Theseus's ship finally returned home to Athens . . .
Home at last! Father will surely be waiting for me atop those cliffs.
Wait!
Where's the white sail?!
On the cliffs above the harbor . . .
No! No! The black sail!
Theseus has failed! He and the others are dead!
The oracle was right all those years ago.
"This son will bring you great unhappiness," she said.
Life is worth nothing without Theseus . . .

Farewell, Athens.
What!?
It can't be!
Nooo!
Father!!

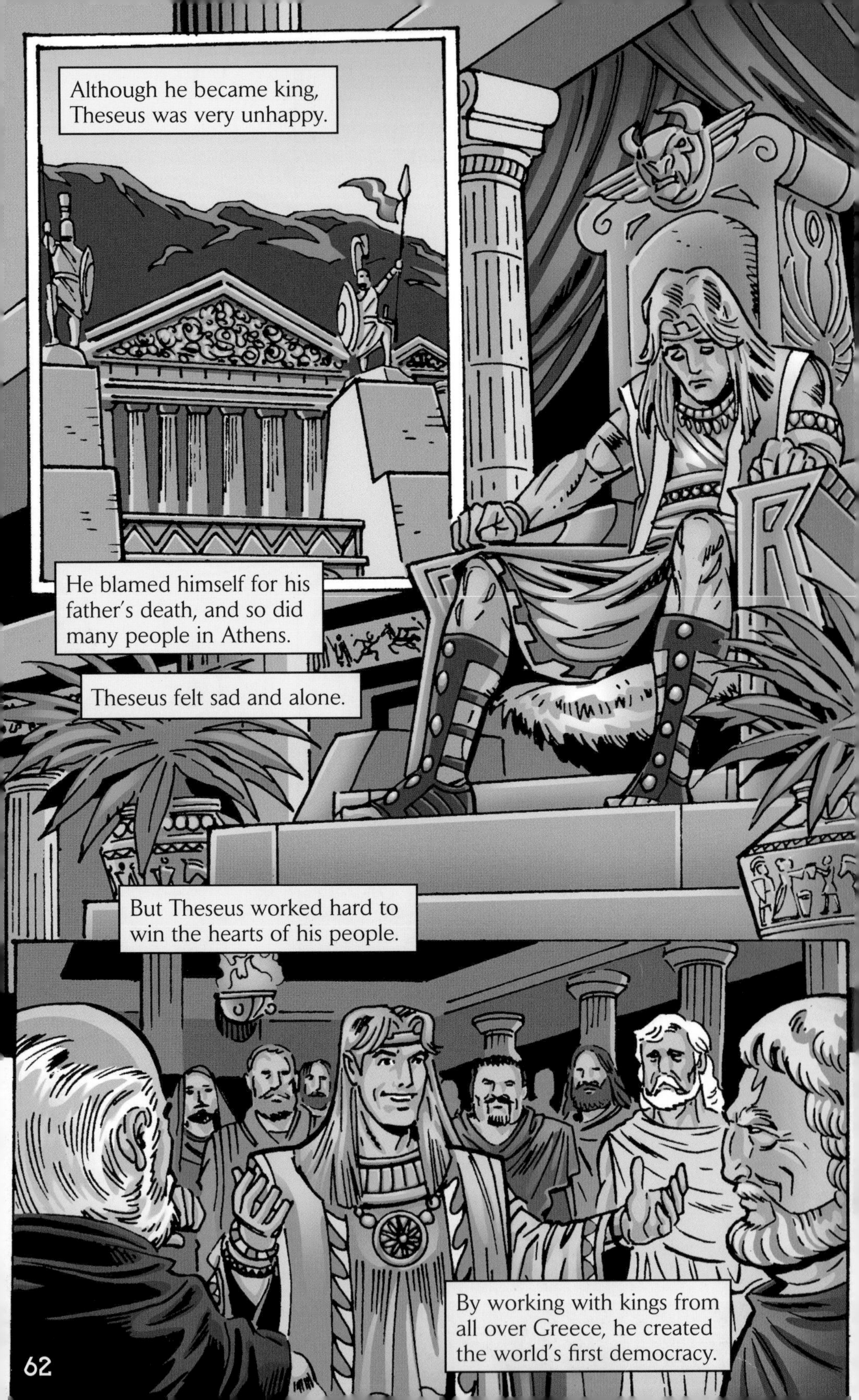
Although he became king, Theseus was very unhappy.
He blamed himself for his father's death, and so did many people in Athens.
Theseus felt sad and alone.
But Theseus worked hard to win the hearts of his people.
By working with kings from all over Greece, he created the world's first democracy.

And to this day, no one will ever forget the battle between Theseus and the Minotaur.

ABOUT THE RETELLING AUTHOR

The career path of Nel Yomtov has taken him from the halls of Marvel Comics, as an editor, writer, and colorist, to the world of toy development. He then became editorial and art director at a children's nonfiction book publisher, and now Nel is a writer and editor of books, websites, and comics for children. A harmonica-honking blues enthusiast, Nel lives in New York with his wife, Nancy. They have a son, Jess.

ABOUT THE ILLUSTRATOR

Tod Smith grew up in Rhode Island. He attended the Joe Kubert School of Cartoon and Graphic Art in Dover, New Jersey. Smith started working in comics in the 1980s, and has been an illustrator for comics and books ever since. He loves to play music in his free time, and when he was in middle school, the Beatles inspired him to start to play the guitar. He lives in Connecticut with his wife, Candace.

GLOSSARY

creature (KREE-chur)—a living being, human or animal

deeds (DEEDZ)—things that are done or need to be done

democracy (di-MOK-ruh-see)—a government that makes decisions through votes

harbor (HAR-bur)—a place where ships stay or unload their cargo

heir (AIR)—a person who is given something upon the death of a friend or relative

oracle (AWR-uh-kuhl)—a person who learns about the future by communicating with the gods

sorceress (SOR-sur-ess)—a female who practices sorcery

sorcery (SOR-sur-ee)—magic involving evil spirits

toll (TOHL)—a charge or tax paid for passage through a bridge or road

torch (TORCH)—a flaming light that can be carried in the hand

villain (VIL-uhn)—a wicked or evil person

THE ORACLE AT DELPHI

Have you ever seen those commercials for psychics on television? Believe it or not, the Greeks had psychics too! They were called the Pythia (PITH-ee-uh) and their leader was called the Oracle. The Pythia were priestesses of Apollo, the god of the sun, in Delphi, Greece. People from all over Greece would visit the Delphic Oracle in hopes of getting a glimpse of the future.

Legend says that Delphi was originally the home of a giant python. Apollo killed the massive serpent and claimed the land as his own, making it a holy site where the Oracle at Delphi would reside. A temple was placed directly on top of a crack in the Earth where odd things had been happening. This is where the Pythia, named after the great python that once lived there, gave their predictions.

When a visitor came to inquire about the future, the Pythia would go downstairs and sit upon a chair placed directly over the crack in the Earth. After sitting there for a while, they would give their prophecies. Most of the time, the Pythia's predictions were vague or impossible to understand. So, other priests would interpret what they said. But really, the priests just made up their own predictions and simply pretended to interpret.

So why did people who went near the crack in the Earth act so strangely? The Greeks thought that this weird behavior meant they had spoken with Apollo through the crack, giving them insight into the future. However, an American archaeologist named John Hale thinks that methane gas leaked out of the crack that the temple was built upon. Long ago, goats that grazed in Delphi would act very strangely when they neared the area. The methane gas may have made them intoxicated, or "drunk" on the gas vapors. This same gas probably made the Pythia act strangely and speak in ways that could not be understood, and it probably affected the priests who interpreted their prophesies too.

For several centuries, the Oracle at Delphi played an important role for rulers across the world. But after a few centuries, less people visited the Oracle. No one knows for certain why people stopped visiting, but some archaeologists believe that the crack in the Earth stopped leaking methane gas, which made the experience of visiting the Oracle less convincing.

DISCUSSION QUESTIONS

1. Theseus had promised to take Ariadne back to Athens with him, but instead he abandoned her on an island. How did his behavior make you feel? What would have been the right thing to do if he didn't love her?

2. Ariadne gave Theseus a ball of string to use to find his way out of the Labyrinth. What are some other ways he could have kept track of his location?

3. Is Theseus responsible for his father's death? Why or why not?

WRITING PROMPTS

1. Deep in the Labyrinth, Theseus comes across the beast-like Minotaur. Imagine you're venturing through the corridors of a Labyrinth. What strange creature awaits you? What does it look like? Write about your monster.

2. On page 13, Medea's chariot is pulled by odd-looking creatures. Write a story explaining how she came to be in possession of such a strange form of transportation.

3. Theseus is visited by the famous hero Hercules. If you could be visited by any person who has ever lived, who would you choose? What would the two of you do together? Write about it.

OTHER BOOKS

Jason and the Golden Fleece

Brave Jason comes to claim his throne, but the old king will not give up his rule so easily. To prove his worth, Jason must find the greatest treasure in the world, the Golden Fleece.

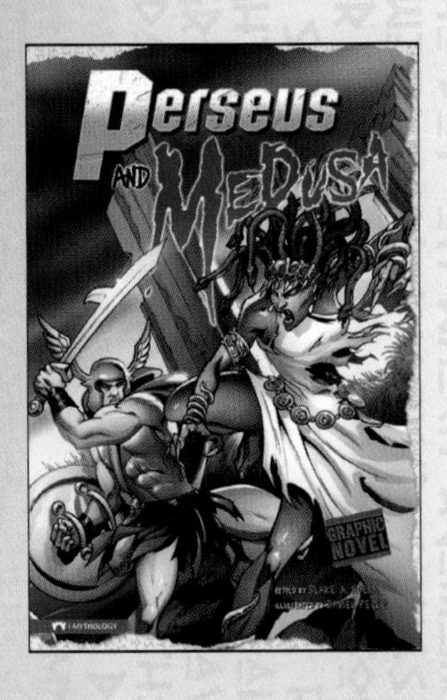

Perseus and Medusa

Young Perseus grows up, unaware of his royal birth. Before he can claim his heritage, the hero is ordered to slay a hideous monster named Medusa, whose gaze turns men into solid stone. How can the youth fight an enemy he cannot even look at?

The Adventures of Hercules

Born of a mortal woman and the king of the gods, Hercules is blessed with extraordinary strength. The goddess Hera commands that the mighty Hercules must undergo twelve incredible tasks to pay for a mistake he made in the past.

The War of the Worlds

In the late 19th century, a cylinder crashes down near London. When George investigates, a Martian activates an evil machine and begins destroying everything in its path! George must find a way to survive a War of the Worlds.

INTERNET SITES

Do you want to know more about subjects related to this book? Or are you interested in learning about other topics? Then check out FactHound, a fun, easy way to find Internet sites.

Our investigative staff has already sniffed out great sites for you!

Here's how to use FactHound:

1. Visit www.facthound.com
2. Select your grade level.
3. To learn more about subjects related to this book, type in the book's ISBN number: **9781434211712**.
4. Click the **Fetch It** button.

FactHound will fetch the best Internet sites for you!